Natalie Coley
Illustrations by David Polalski

The Horror Trilogy

Read if You Dare

A collection of 3 short, spooky stories designed to scare even the
strongest of victims.

Bumblebee Books
London

A CIP catalogue record for this title is
available from the British Library.

ISBN: 978-1-83934-020-8

Bumblebee Books is an imprint of
Olympia Publishers.

First Published in 2021

Bumblebee Books
Tallis House
2 Tallis Street
London
EC4Y 0AB

Printed in Great Britain

www.olympiapublishers.com

About the Author

Natalie Coley is a teacher from Leicestershire who has a passion for travel, sport and books. She was encouraged to write from a young age by her family and teachers and would always gather the family around to hear her latest stories as a child. Her first published book 'The Horror Trilogy' was inspired by her student's love of spooky stories and a series of wild, yet terrifying dreams!

IN THE SHALLOWS

Come. Do it.
Explore these waters.
But only horrors lie here,
In the shallows.

In the Shallows

Squelching and with an unnaturally, twisted movement, the long, green, slimy tentacle constricted itself around the ankle of its unsuspecting victim. Within a split second, another skilfully slithered, slipped and wrapped itself around the agape mouth ensnaring an escaping scream. As the waves drew their breath back towards the sea, the victim was taken in one large, slimy gulp.

In the midday sun, the children splashed and played along the shore of the beach. It was summer and time to have fun. Parents basked on their sunbeds, reading a magazine or catching up on the latest news on their social media feed while absorbing the sun's hot rays.

One mother in particular, her first time bringing her children to the beach, was noticeably anxious. She watched her children, both boys, like a hawk as they crashed along the shore line. Sat  bolt upright, uncomfortably positioned in her straw, brimmed hat and shades she protected her young. She may easily be named 'over-protective' in her meerkat-like stance, but the motherly instincts inside her would not let her settle.

Suddenly, a large object swished and flapped in front of the mother. Sand kicked up into her face and her vision became obscured by the four figures before her. Anxiety struck through her as her watch over her children was hindered. Hastily, she swept the sand from her eyes. It scratched uncomfortably against her skin. Annoyed at this obstruction, the mother gathered her towel and moved a metre to the left. She made no effort to hide her annoyance at the family who had just ruined her perfect spot.

Panic ripped through her chest. The beach became a blur. Her eyes scrambled to spot the bright, red swimming trunks of her two boys. She could not see them. As her pulse rose, a prickling heat tormented her neck and chest.

A squelching sound interrupted her terror. From over her shoulder a wet, slimy tentacle slid. The mother let out a small scream. 'Get that off me!' she yelped, cringing away from the cold, unpleasant sliminess of the seaweed. The boys fell to the floor laughing. The mother, less than amused at her children's idea of a joke, recovered from her panic and called it a day. Reluctantly, the family of three went back to their hotel room for dinner.

The eldest sibling awoke at 9pm. He could not say what had woken him. As he lay in the hotel room bed, he thought about the beach and the sea and the wonderful time he and his younger brother had shared. They would be leaving for home tomorrow morning and the thought of leaving made him question whether he had made the most of his holiday. As silently as he was able to, the boy tip-toed to his brother's room.

As he peered over his brother's bed, he could see that he was already awake. He raised his finger to his lips to hush him and beckoned for his younger brother to follow. Never one to miss an adventure, the boy followed his brother out of the hotel room door and down to the beach.

The waves hissed against the silence of the night. The boys sat quietly by the shore and watched as the waves drew back and forth, inhaling and exhaling peacefully and rhythmically.

Sat quietly, the boys could hear an unusual squelching and slipping sound that they had not noticed during the buzz and commotion of the day. They strained to hear it. It was unlike anything they had heard before. The sound drew the youngest closer to the lapping waves. Fascinated, he teased his fingers through the shallow waters which were full of green, slimy seaweed. He clasped his fingers around some and a shiver passed over him at the surprising chill of the waters.

The eldest gazed back at the dancing lights of the hotel which were not far from the beach. His day-dreaming was interrupted by a strange slurping sound. If it were not so silent out on the beach, the momentary sound, almost like a sun cream bottle was being squeezed, would have been easily missed.

The boy turned around. He could not see anyone.

Scanning the shore line, sure that his brother was playing one of his usual practical jokes, the boys eyes landed on a black mass.

Sniggering and sneaking, the eldest boy approached the mass. As he drew closer, he could see that the mass was moving. Were his eyes playing tricks or was the mass glistening? Not in a way that brings happiness or makes you smile with pleasure. No. The glistening was like that of light dancing off a trail of mucous left by a snail.

The eldest boy picked up a stick ready to poke his unsuspecting brother. He jabbed the stick at the mass. Taken off guard by the slipperiness and fluid state of the mass, the boy was thrown off balance and sank into the pool of green, slick weeds. Disturbed by the fishy smell and jelly-like feeling of his surroundings, the boy tried to stand up. As he began to move, he felt something slither over his chest. Panicked, the boy tried to stand again. Another tendril slipped its way over his mouth while another entwined around his legs. In the silent night, the boy's ears were filled with the sounds of slipping and oozing.

The sea let out a breath. The boy was surrounded by icy cold waters. The boy attempted to thrash and scream. The sea inhaled. With one swift movement, the sea recalled its limbs and the beach was empty once more.

STRAW MEN

We wait do we,
With limbs of straw.
With eyes aglow,
A smile that lures.
Dance with us,
Then, harvest our young.
In the fields we wait,
We are unstrung.

Straw Men

It was the 31st October 2019 and that could only mean one thing: pumpkin picking day! Lucy threw on her coat, hat and gloves and pulled her mother towards their silver VW Passat. Lucy had been waiting for this evening since the end of summer and could not wait to choose a pumpkin to carve. With greatly less enthusiasm than her daughter, Carol put on her own coat and reluctantly stepped out into the cold October air. Turning on the engine and ramping up the in-car heating to full blast the pair set off to Farmer Jo's Pumpkin Picking Spook-tacular!

When they arrived, Carol drove the car into the muddy field and instantly regretted not bringing her wellington boots. As they pulled up in the muddy patch of a carpark, Lucy leapt from the vehicle and bounced with excitement. Carol grasped her daughters hand and walked towards the bright walkway leading them towards the main event. She sighed as she glanced down at her white trainers and resigned them to the mud. The pair walked down the lit walk-way which was lined with spooky pumpkin-headed scarecrows. Each had a different, hand-carved face which glowed from within with a small light.

At eight years old, Lucy was amazed by the towering figures and made a mental note of her favourite which she would try to copy onto her own pumpkin later. She settled on a spooky fellow. He had straw roughly protruding from all four limbs. On top of his dungarees-dressed torso sat a chunky round head which displayed a wonky, jagged smile. His triangular eyes glowed burnt orange in colour. The light danced from within them which gave the impression as though eyes were following her as she continued with her mother down the path.

At the end of the lit walk-way, Carol pulled out her purse to pay the entry fee. Uninterested in the exchange, Lucy glanced back over her shoulder. She jumped. Not at something she had seen, but at something that she had not. A heavy, scratchy hand thudded on her shoulder. Lucy let out a scream. As she quickly turned around, a tall figure dressed in dungarees with an orange round face looked down at her. Her eyes cast down towards the straw protruding from his limbs and she cowered back towards her mother.

'Sorry about that!' laughed the figure. 'Didn't mean to scare you. Welcome to our Spook-tactular night!'

'But he is gone!' is all Lucy could form through her quivering lips as she looked back down the walkway.

'Don't let the lights play tricks on your dear,' said the man in costume. 'It's a dark evening but we are all here to have fun. Relax and enjoy yourself!'

Lucy nodded and Carol thanked the man. After walking a few steps out of hearing distance of the man, Carol whispered, 'What was that all about?'

'It's that pumpkin scarecrow we were looking at earlier! He's gone!' shrieked Lucy.

'What are you talking about?' asked Carol in an annoyed tone. 'He is right there. You have just embarrassed me in front of my friend with this silliness. Now come on.'

With that Lucy was marched on by her mother. Lucy, once again, glanced back over her shoulder. She jumped again. Her mother was right. He was there. You may think that Lucy was reassured by this. Maybe she would have been, if it were not for the fact that Lucy was almost certain that the figure was closer than before.

Lucy decided to put the strange occurrence out of her mind. After all, she did not want to upset her mother. They walked down to the main field which was lit by pumpkin-shaped lanterns. The light danced across the field which was lined with pumpkins ready to be picked.

After fifteen minutes of looking for the perfect pumpkin, Lucy finally settled on one. It was the perfect size; large but not too heavy to carry. It was the perfect colour; bright orange and with no discolouring, and not too far from the car so that Lucy's little arms could carry it. As she bent down to pick up the pumpkin, she heard shouting from across the field. Carol stood up and Lucy saw it was the man that they had spoken to earlier – Mum's friend. 'You carry on, dear. I am just going to go and speak to Jo. I won't be far away.'

Lucy did not mind and continued to kneel down to retrieve her pumpkin. As she knelt in the muddy field, she heard a squelch a few yards behind her. She startled at the noise but continued to retrieve her pumpkin. 'Help me carry it please, Mum,' she said. There was no reply. 'Come on, Mum,' she complained. There was still no reply. Lucy lifted her head and spun around in the mud to look at her mother. Her jaw dropped. As she turned around she lifted her gaze from the bottom of the dungarees, to the messy straw limbs, to the glowing wonky smile to the burning, dancing eyes. It was him!

Lucy fell back into the mud and thudded against something which made a scrunching sound as her head fell against it. She looked up into the leering, carved gaze of the pumpkin's hollow face. She tried to scream but no sound escaped. She scrambled to her feet, sliding on the slippery mud. As Lucy tried to find her escape, she took in the scene on the field once more. The field, once empty apart from the rows of pumpkins, was now surrounded by row upon row of pumpkin-faced scarecrows encircling her.

Overwhelmed with fear at the sight of the glowing eyes, which followed her every move, Lucy attempted to run. She found herself unable to move. Suckered in by her boots she was trapped in the mud! Her eyes darted from wonky smile to wonky smile. From gleaning eye to gleaning eye. The field of scarecrows began to spin before her until she found herself in total darkness.

Lucy awoke to rumbling and a warm blowing on her forehead. Confused, Lucy slowly opened her eyes and looked up to her mother who was driving the car. As always, the car was uncomfortably hot. 'What?' Was all Lucy could manage to utter. Her mother gave her a look which was filled with concern and disappointment. 'What happened back there? You really embarrassed me today in front of Jo.'

Lucy gasped. She suddenly remembered the events of the evening. The wonky smiles. The gleaning eyes. The scrunching. The squelching. The field of scarecrows. Being stuck in the mud. Her heart raced. 'Didn't you see the scarecrows?' Lucy said in a mixture of amazement and fear.

'Stop it now. I have had enough of your silliness today,' her mother replied in a frustrated tone.

Lucy did not say another word. She stared out of the window for the rest of the journey. Surely she could not have been the only one to see the scarecrows? Surely her eyes had not been playing tricks on her in the dark field of dancing lights?

Later that evening, Lucy settled into bed. As she drew her curtains, a flickering caught her eye from down in the garden below. Lucy staggered back from the window in shock. Leering up at her were ten pairs of hollow, dancing eyes, with wonky smiles and messy straw limbs. Lucy did not dare look again. She leapt into bed, hiding and quivering under the covers.

From beneath her quilt, she could make out the flickering light refracting through her window which cast taunting orange flames across her bed. She could hear the unmistakable scrunch, scrunch scrunching of straw. The presence of the straw men was almost tangible. Scrunch, scrunch, scrunch. The dancing lights grew larger. SCRUNCH, SCRUNCH, SCRUNCH. The scrunching grew louder.

SCRUNCH. SCRUNCH. SCRUNCH.

THE TREEHOUSE

In the boughs of the oak,
I stand strong.
Within my walls of timber,
Memories made, fond.
Though, I house a secret,
A presence fills my structure.
Within my walls of timber,
Your resolve may fracture.

The Treehouse

Adam and Jack were bored. Looking out of the bedroom window, on the overcast day, the boys sighed. 'I'm bored!' Adam sighed.

The bedroom door flew open. 'If I hear you two say those words again there will be trouble!' exclaimed Dad, exasperated. 'Grab your coats and meet me near the tree over the road.' Dad shut the door. The brothers exchanged a glance, shrugged and trundled across the road to the field.

As they made their way towards their meeting point, they took in the large, gnarly oak with its impressive, large branches spanning overhead. Beneath the oak, Dad was hammering planks of wood together. 'Now you two. Us Smiths don't do bored. I heard you pair moaning and I couldn't take any more! I will show you what we did when we were younger, when we were bored.' He gestured towards his hammer and planks of wood. 'We are going to build a treehouse!' It may have been the sheer boredom that had taken its toll on the two nine-year-olds, but the boys found themselves throwing themselves into their father's idea.

The boys spent the day making the impressive structure. They followed the lead from their enthusiastic father and hammered, nailed, balanced and clambered their way around the trees creaky, yet sturdy branches.

Crash! Crash! Crash! The threesome dropped from the tree and stood back to admire their work. It was fantastic! In the bow of the oak rested a cubed room with a triangular leaning roof. Their father had also cleverly installed a small window which Adam noticed had a great view of his bedroom window. He could even see Jack's and his bunkbeds from it!

Exhausted, the three staggered back to the house. 'Now boys,' Dad began. The boys exchanged a look and a sigh which meant that they knew all too well that a lecture was coming. Ignoring this unconcealed exchange, Dad continued, 'Don't you let me hear you moaning about being bored again! That thing we have built up there is anything you want it to be! It can be a spaceship fallen from outer space. It can be a cave to be explored! It can be…'

'OK Dad!' the boys interrupted simultaneously. 'We get the message.'

With a small smirk, Dad led the boys inside for supper and a well-deserved glass of orange juice before bed. When eight o'clock came the boys were sent to bed as usual and darkness fell over the bedroom.

Adam awoke in the night. Never one to make it through the night, he slipped out of the top bunk, slipped on his dinosaur slippers and shuffled to the bathroom. It did not occur to him until he sat on the toilet seat that he had not needed to turn the light on. He was already able to see. In a groggy, late-night state Adam thought nothing more. He washed his hands, shuffled across the landing and returned to his bedroom. It was then that he saw it. Startled, he rushed to his brother who was still sleeping peacefully on the bottom bunk. 'Jack... Jack,' he whispered. 'Someone has stolen our treehouse.'

'Wh... what?' Responded Jack, sleepily.

'Come and see!' urged Adam. With that he pulled his brother to the bedroom window. Sure enough, from within the treehouse, a torch glowed. The boys stood for a second, shocked at the cheek of someone stealing their treehouse! As the pair watched, a shadow crossed the small treehouse window. The boys gasped in shock. How dare someone steal their treehouse!

The boys observed as the figure moved from side to side; seemingly circling the structure. The movement of the intruder caused the light to flash making it momentarily difficult to see into the treehouse. As the boys wiped their eyes and squinted back toward the house, a cold blade of ice struck through their chests. The person had stopped moving. Clear as day in front of the still torchlight, they could see the figure was staring back at them. Staring directly into the bedroom window!

Now that the figure was still, the boys could see that they were cloaked, with their hood up so that only their eyes could be seen as the torch-light cast across their face. As the boys looked back, the figure slowly raised a bony arm and waved mockingly.

Adam's original feelings of fear turned to rage. 'How dare they!' He turned to his brother, 'Come on, Jack! I don't care who they are; they are NOT taking out treehouse. We spent all day making it and it's OURS!'

'I… I don't know, Adam.' Jack replied uneasily. 'I don't like this. Who do you know that would stand in a treehouse alone at night, watching our house! It's too weird. I don't like it.'

'Don't be such a wimp!' Adam scalded. 'People need to know that they can't mess with the Smiths and get away with it!' Always the stronger of the two, Adam got his own way and before he knew it, Jack was being dragged in his slippers down to the treehouse.

As they crossed the road, they noticed that the treehouse was dark. The light, that was once making the treehouse visible, was out. 'Maybe they have gone?' Jack questioned hopefully. The cold night air made his hairs stand on end and his knee length dressing gown left his ankles uncomfortably exposed to the mid-night chill of the air. Seeming to ignore his brother, Adam pressed on. With his jaw set and forehead crumpled in determination and anger Adam pulled his brother to the base of the tree.

Maybe Jack was right. The night was silent apart from the whit-wooing of an owl and the creaking and moaning of the ancient, impressive oak. While Adam seemed oblivious to the eeriness of the night, Jack's senses became attuned to the groaning and creaking. The swishing and crunching. The shrieking and scurrying of a nearby creature. The damp smell of the Earth. The longer they stood under the boughs of the oak, the more vigilant his senses became to the uncomfortable presence of the night.

The boys' senses were shocked back to the tree as the light of the torch struck back on. Jack stumbled back in shock but Adam's jaw tightened further and he began to ascend into the branches of the tree. 'You up there!' he called angrily into the torch light. 'Get out of our tree!' his calls were responded to only with further creaking and groaning as he advanced up the trees old limbs. Jack watched as his brother's legs clambered over the entrance to the treehouse. He heard a gasp from within the structure which ignited a natural brotherly instinct to protect his twin.

Jack scrambled and scraped up the trunk of the tree. Cutting his forearms and knees, as he struggled to make purchase with the moist bark in his slippers, Jack cautiously dragged himself over the ledge of the treehouse entrance. He peered into the torch light.

Initially, he was blinded by the surprisingly intense light. His senses hampered, he felt a bolt of fear strike through his chest once again. He could hear footsteps circling, scurrying around the torch. As his vision adjusted to the light, he was shocked to see only one figure before him. A hand stretched toward his own. Adam pulled his brother to his feet on the sturdy platform they had created earlier that day. 'Ha!' exclaimed Adam. 'I told you! No-one messes with the Smiths! Must've scared them off whoever they were.' A flood of relief washed over Jack. Thank goodness he didn't have to deal with the intruder. Fighting was not Jack's forte.

Unfortunately, Jack's relief was short-lived. As the boys sat in the base of the treehouse, leaning smugly on the windowsill of the make-shift window, they saw a light strike on. The shock was so great that, as Jack turned to grasp his brother in fright, he saw fear take over his brother's expression for the first time. Opposite them, in their own bedroom window, a hooded figure stared back.

Still as the night the figure stood. The bedroom light was a striking contrast to the black of the hooded cloak. As it had done before, the figure slowly raised its bony arm and waved chillingly in the boys' direction.

All of a sudden, the pair became acutely aware of the cold night air whistling through the window at them. They could feel the heat of the pair of eyes of the figure burning into theirs. The brothers did not dare to break eye-contact; the three beings stared at one another. The boys' breath fogged the freezing air as they panted with fear.

Suddenly, the bedroom door pushed open behind the intruder. It was Dad! The boys took in their father's confused expression made clear by the light of the room and a face they knew only too well. The curtains closed and the room went dark. The boys were left speechless and in shock. What had just happened? Who was in their bedroom? Was Dad OK? What should they do?

Originally too scared to move, the boys sat staring silently into the darkness. After a while, slowly and uneasily the pair clambered back down the tree, shuffled across the road and re-entered their house.

The house was silent; not unusual for this hour of night. If it were not for the events that had just unfolded before them this would feel perfectly normal. Except, they had unfolded. Except, it didn't feel normal at all. As they approached the landing, they could see no light escaping from the space underneath their bedroom door.

The pair, feeling un-daring at this time, made a turn for their parents' room. As they shuffled from the bottom of the quilt to the top, they nestled themselves between the two figures in their parents' bed. Shaking and unnerved, the boys settled there.

They got little sleep that night. As they lay in the bed, Jack became acutely aware of the figures laying either side of him. One was unmistakably the safe, comforting figure of his brother. The other, he realised, felt less so.

Printed in Great Britain
by Amazon